T0375506

RETRIBUTION

Also by Robert S. Felber

Choices
Heartache: Poems of Love, Sorrow, and Remorse
The Harrises: The Lives and Loves of an American Family

RETRIBUTION

Robert S. Felber

Copyright © 2007 by Robert S. Felber.

Library of Congress Control Number:		2007901930
ISBN:	Hardcover	978-1-4257-6485-2
	Softcover	978-1-4257-6470-8

All rights reserved. No part of this book may be reproduced or transmitted in any form or by any means, electronic or mechanical, including photocopying, recording, or by any information storage and retrieval system, without permission in writing from the copyright owner.

This is a work of fiction. Names, characters, places and incidents either are the product of the author's imagination or are used fictitiously, and any resemblance to any actual persons, living or dead, events, or locales is entirely coincidental.

This book was printed in the United States of America.

To order additional copies of this book, contact:
Xlibris Corporation
1-888-795-4274
www.Xlibris.com
Orders@Xlibris.com
36119

To the victims.

ACKNOWLEDGMENTS

I would like to thank Ruth Gordon and Madeline Buckley for reviewing the manuscript. I also appreciate Ruth Gordon's help in selecting the cover artwork.

If you prick us, do we not bleed? If you tickle us, do we not laugh? If you poison us, do we not die? And if you wrong us, shall we not revenge?

—William Shakespeare, *The Merchant of Venice* (1596-1597), 3.1.65

CHAPTER 1

Jack was about to roll from his back to his side when he thought he heard a groan. Instantly, he was wide awake. Over the years, he had learned to be alert for Gretchen's nightmares. He raised himself on one elbow and looked down at her beautiful face. She was breathing heavily, with her eyes still closed, as her expression became increasingly anguished. Then, reverting to her native German, she uttered, "Nein, nein, bitte" ("No, no, please").

Jack touched Gretchen's cheek and gently shook her shoulder with his other hand. He said softly, "Wake up, baby. Everything is fine. You're safe." Suddenly, her eyes opened. Upon seeing Jack, she exclaimed, "Jack, oh Jack!" and reached for him.

Jack got up on his knees and tenderly lifted Gretchen in his arms. He kissed the side of her head and repeated, "You're safe." Then he added, "I'm here to protect you. Don't worry."

Those were basically the same words Jack had used to comfort Gretchen when he had first met her. At the time, since she knew no English, she hadn't understood what they meant. Nevertheless, his tone had been soothing.

Just as back then, Gretchen now went limp in Jack's arms. Only this time, it was voluntary. It wasn't because she had no strength to sit up by herself. With her head resting on Jack's neck and shoulder, she said, "It was about him again." Jack responded, "I know; I pretty much figured that."

Gretchen let go of Jack and lowered her head to the pillow as she looked up at him longingly. Jack told her, "We don't have to. It's probably not a good time." Gretchen replied, "I want to. I love you, Jack." She gladly offered herself to the man who had been her savior years earlier and had since given her a renewed sense of life.

CHAPTER 2

Although the O'Brien twins, Anthony and Patrick, weren't identical, they did bear a strong resemblance to each other. An additional similarity was that they were both in law enforcement. That had been a tradition on the Irish side of their family for generations. Also, rumor had it that one of their Italian ancestors had been a police officer in the old country.

In deference to both ethnic sides of the family, one brother had been given a typical Irish first name and the other a typical Italian first name. Actually, the twins were only twenty-five percent Italian. Their maternal grandmother Gretchen was a German Jew who had lost her entire previous family in the Second World War. When, as a war bride, she had married into the Tangredi clan, she was quickly absorbed as one of their own.

Tony, as Anthony was usually called, was having a successful career with the FBI. His current duties included tracking down missing persons and terrorist suspects. Patrick was a detective in New York City's police department. He was exceptionally well educated and was often involved in special assignments.

By 2003, both brothers, at age 30, had advanced rather quickly within their agencies. Each of them was quite competent and highly regarded.

Neither Tony nor Patrick was married. Tony was more of a player than his brother. Patrick had once been engaged, but the relationship had ended suddenly. It left him with a broken heart. However, after going through the grief cycle, he recovered and was back to his old self.

Their mother Angela was concerned that her two boys were still unmarried in their thirties. Their sister Theresa was already engaged at age twenty. There were no other siblings.

Tony and Patrick were very protective of Theresa. They had her fiancé totally intimidated. He was reluctant to touch her in front of them. They got a big kick out of that even though it upset Theresa.

They had always teased her. When she was younger, she would sometimes cry. Then they would feel guilty and have to face the punishment from their parents. Theresa still occasionally got annoyed at her brothers, but she could count on them for anything. She was as crazy about them as they were about her.

Part of her brothers' protectiveness was due to Theresa's good looks. They knew how guys thought, and they didn't like them thinking that way about their baby sister. Actually, they were both glad that she was engaged. Her going out with several different guys would have really had them worried.

Theresa and their mother, Angela, looked so much like Angela's mother, Gretchen. The boys and Theresa had always adored Grandma Gretchen. One couldn't help but feel close to her. She was so loving.

But there had always been a sadness about her. As her grandchildren grew older, they realized that it had to do with her experience during the Holocaust. Although nothing much was mentioned about it, they knew that Grandma Gretchen had met Grandpa Jack when his Army outfit had liberated the concentration camp where she was a prisoner. She was the only member of her family who had survived. She had been dying, too, but Grandpa Jack nursed her back to health, and they fell in love.

It was in 2001 when Grandpa Jack had died at age eighty. Fortunately, he had been relatively healthy until a massive stroke ended his life.

Needless to say, Grandma Gretchen had taken it hard. After 56 years of marriage, she had lost not just her love, but the person she practically worshiped.

Angela and her husband Pete had Gretchen move in with them. There was no way that they could leave her alone. At age seventy-six, she would have felt again like that terrified girl her beloved Jack had once rescued.

Angela appreciated how caring Pete was toward her mother. Behind that tough Irish cop exterior, he was kind and considerate. That's what had made Angela fall in love with him in the first place.

Not surprisingly, the widowed Gretchen would drift into periods of depression. It was as if a piece of her were missing. The last time Gretchen had been like this was when Angela was a little girl. As the only child, Angela had been close to both of her parents, but she had spent most of her time with her mother. Angela remembered often seeing Gretchen crying and then wiping away the tears when she realized her daughter had noticed. The only time Gretchen had ever seemed truly happy was when she was with her darling Jack. Away from him, she felt unsafe.

It didn't take long for Gretchen to deteriorate. Without Jack, she had lost her reason for living. Even the love of her daughter and grandchildren wasn't enough. She had no appetite and became careless with her medications. Within a year and a half, she was dead.

The official cause of death was pneumonia. But everyone close to her knew that Gretchen had died from a broken heart. At least now she could be reunited with her dear Jack.

Years ago, Gretchen had converted to Catholicism. The Holocaust had made her lose her faith in God, but she wanted to someday be buried next to her husband. She got her wish as she was put to rest beside him at the Tangredi family plot in the local Catholic cemetery.

CHAPTER 3

Pete was sitting on the living room couch. His attention was divided between the newspaper and the ball game on TV. It was another casual day for him. Just about all of them were since his recent retirement from the New York City police force. Sometimes he missed the action, but he didn't regret leaving the job. He enjoyed spending the extra time with Angela. And he could vicariously live through his two sons, Tony and Patrick. He loved discussing their careers with them. He was pleased that they were both doing well.

He could also indulge his little girl, Theresa. Of course, she wasn't little anymore. She was a grown woman who was about to be married. Pete had mixed feelings about that. Naturally, he was happy for her, but deep down, he hated to lose his baby. And it was hard to accept that she was sexually active with her fiancé. But that's life. His father-in-law, Jack, must have felt the same way about Angela and him.

Pete started to wonder why things were so quiet. Usually, Angela would be moving about, cleaning or rearranging things. And he could always count on her scolding him for leaving crumbs or stains somewhere. He knew she wasn't joking when she would tell him how his being around the house drove her crazy.

Pete looked at his watch. By now, Angela should have been sending him to the supermarket with her seemingly endless list of items to purchase. That had become his regular assignment. Angela told him it was how he could make himself useful. But she said it with a twinkle in her eye. Quite often, she would accompany him. She teased Pete by saying that she wanted to make sure he wouldn't screw things up.

Pete realized that his two sons inherited their sarcastic sense of humor from their mother. Unfortunately for their baby sister, she had taken the brunt of it as a child. But gradually, she had come to recognize her brothers' playfulness.

Pete finally decided to go upstairs to find Angela. He was getting worried. When he turned off the TV, the entire house was silent. His police officer's instincts started to take over. The adrenalin was pumping as he ran up the steps. He purposely left his mind blank. He was afraid to think anything. But he had a nagging sense of guilt for not checking on Angela sooner. How much time had gone by since he had heard a peep out of her?

Pete exhaled a sigh of relief when he saw Angela sitting at the desk in their bedroom. Her back was to him, but he could tell that she was all right. He tapped the door and said "Hey, Angie." There was no response. If he didn't know better, he would have thought she was deaf. He banged harder on the door and asked, "Angela, what's up?"

Angela turned her head toward Pete. Tears were streaming down her face. Pete again asked, "What's up?" Only this time, there was deep concern in his voice. His first fear was that something had happened to one of the kids. But the phone hadn't rung all day. And Angela didn't get involved with computers and e-mail.

Walking toward his ailing wife, Pete inquired, "Baby, what's wrong?" Now, Angela started to sob. He repeated, "What's wrong?" Her sobs turned into a virtual wail. When he put Angela's head on his shoulder, his shirt became soaked by her tears.

She tried to talk, but all that came out of her were incoherent guttural sounds. She couldn't catch her breath. Pete raised her to a standing position, saying nothing as he tightly held her.

Then he noticed a stack of papers on the desk. He was about to look closer when Angela finally was able to speak. She managed to let out, "My poor mother, my poor darling mother." Pete sensed the significance of the sheets of paper. He saw that the information on them was handwritten. He also recognized the neat, attractive penmanship of his late mother-in-law.

CHAPTER 4

Tony was wrapping things up in his office at FBI headquarters in Washington, D.C. It was one of the few times he was going to leave work early. It was Friday afternoon, and he was looking forward to a relaxing weekend for a change.

There was finally a lull in his workload, and he had no social activities planned. He had decided that the two latest women in his life weren't for him. One wasn't really his type, and the other was practically engaged to a Marine Corps officer stationed overseas. She hadn't divulged that little fact to Tony until after he had gone to bed with her.

As he was about to get up from his desk, Tony yawned and stretched his arms over his head. Then he let out a "Damn it" in response to the ringing of his phone. He thought to himself, "There goes my quiet weekend." He anticipated the latest national crisis or task force needing his attention.

Tony picked up the handset and identified himself. To his relief, he heard Patrick's voice saying, "Hi, bro, it's me." Tony responded cheerfully, "Hey, Paddy boy!" as he settled in for a pleasant keeping-in-touch conversation with his brother. They didn't get to see each other very often since Tony's transfer to Washington, and Tony missed Patrick. They had always been two peas in a pod.

Then Tony sensed concern in his twin's voice when Patrick asked, "Listen, big guy, do you think you can get up here this weekend?" Tony's immediate response was, "Is everybody okay?" Patrick informed him that everyone was fine, but that their mother was "kind of upset about something." When Tony asked for more details, Patrick told him that it would be best if he could see things for himself. It was too complicated to explain over the phone.

At Tony's insistence, Patrick reassured him that nothing had happened to their parents or Theresa. Then Tony said that he was on his way.

Patrick had done all that he could to contain his emotions during his phone call to Tony. In addition to the tears Patrick had shed upon reading their grandmother's writings, he was seething with anger. He was anxious for his brother to get up to speed. Tony could then use his contacts and expertise in determining the whereabouts of one Heinrich Schmidt, the commandant of their grandmother's concentration camp. Hopefully, the bastard was still alive. Patrick wanted the satisfaction of personally repaying the man for his grandmother's suffering. He knew that his brother would concur.

When Tony arrived at his parents' house, he again inquired if everyone was all right. Patrick and his folks confirmed that everybody was fine. But he was still uneasy. He had been filled with consternation the entire trip up to New York.

Tony looked around and asked, "Where's Theresa?" His mother answered, "She's with Billy. Where else?" Then she added, "They're moving in together." She knew that would upset Tony, as it did his father and brother. But it was an indirect way of assuring him that nothing terrible had happened. Tony was about to protest, but his mother's instincts had been correct. He let it pass as he realized how relieved he was. That should be the worst news that he would hear about his baby sister.

Now more relaxed, Tony asked, "So what's going on?" His father told him that they had come upon some papers left by Grandma Gretchen, describing her experience in the concentration camp. Patrick interjected, "You should go upstairs alone and read them. But brace yourself, bro, and bring plenty of tissues." Angela broke down and sobbed. Tony was in a daze.

Tony heeded Patrick's advice to prepare himself for something unpleasant. But when he went through Grandma Gretchen's papers, he was overwhelmed. It must have been unbearably painful for poor Grandma to re-live that suffering.

In spite of how disgusting it all was, Tony remained focused. He even re-examined certain sections. It was one thing to read a book or see a documentary about the Holocaust. But this was an account, given in excruciating detail, by someone he loved. Besides Grandma, his other relatives had suffered so. He was filled with sadness and anger.

Unlike his mother, father, and brother, Tony didn't shed a tear as he perused his grandmother's memoir. It wasn't until he had finished that he released his emotion and wept like a baby.

Tony knew why Patrick had been eager for him to see Grandma's writings. Tony was already reviewing in his mind the steps he would take to ascertain the status of Heinrich Schmidt. He shared Patrick's hope that the monster was still alive. By Tony's calculations, Schmidt would be in his early to mid eighties.

CHAPTER 5

Gretchen had written down her experiences in chronological order without referring to specific dates. Understandably, she had lost track of time during her inhumane incarceration. And she had started recording her recollections decades later. But it was clear that she had spent years in the concentration camp.

Gretchen had attached a note to her package, explaining that she had put to paper her horrible memories so that her daughter and grandchildren would know about her past. She loved them more than life itself, but she previously had parents and siblings whom she also loved. Her losing them and the way that they had perished would always haunt her. She wanted her new family to appreciate that her previous family were kin, their own flesh and blood.

Tony thought how ironic it was that Gretchen, in spite of those strong feelings, had always found it too difficult to talk about her past, except to her darling Jack. As painful as writing her memoir must have also been, hopefully it had served as a catharsis.

Gretchen's note had been very moving. But the worst was yet to come. It all began when she, her parents, and two brothers arrived at the camp. Gretchen, at sixteen years old, was the middle child. Her brothers were fourteen and nineteen.

Upon their arrival, they were assembled with the rest of their group so that the commandant could "introduce" himself. He was surprisingly young, only in his early twenties. In addition, he was quite haughty and conceited. As Gretchen and the rest of her poor lot would find out, he was also sadistic.

Standing there, looking handsome in his immaculate uniform, Heinrich Schmidt "welcomed" his new "guests." He bragged that it was unusual at his age to hold such a responsible position, and that he had attained it because of exceptional intelligence and ability. He had no intention of allowing his perfect record to become blemished. His tone then changed from falsely polite to threatening.

Schmidt warned that he would not tolerate any disobedience or laziness. He wasn't going to let lowly scum interfere with his advancement. Then he walked past the new prisoners, staring each one in the face. When Schmidt got to Gretchen, he stopped and looked up and down her body. He smiled and said, "Ah, a pretty little Jew." He glanced at some of the guards and stated, "Not bad." He and the guards chuckled. Gretchen was petrified.

It was at this point in his reading that Tony put down the papers. He sensed what would eventually be coming. He had to brace himself for it. He reflected on Gretchen's note that said her two families were kin. He imagined Theresa, her grandmother's look-alike, in Gretchen's place. Under the Nazis' perverted racial theories, Tony and his siblings, as one-fourth Jews, would have been destined for a concentration camp. Never before had Tony identified with his Jewish background. But now, picturing his baby sister in his grandmother's predicament, and picturing himself and Patrick in the place of Grandma's brothers, helpless to do anything about it, he identified completely. His grandmother's account of her ordeal was becoming more and more personal. His blood was boiling. And he hadn't even gotten to the bad parts yet.

Tony picked up the papers to resume his reading. He took a deep breath as he plowed ahead to learn about his grandmother's nightmare.

CHAPTER 6

It was Gretchen's second day at the camp when she was escorted into Schmidt's office. It was as if she had passed from one world into another. She instantly stepped from the stark surroundings of a concentration camp into a luxurious setting.

Schmidt asked Gretchen if she was hungry. Of course, he knew she was. He pointed to a table with lots of food. He told her she could have as much as she wanted. But since she was an animal, she should eat like one. He instructed the two guards to undress Gretchen. Her body stiffened with fear. It was the first time, but certainly not the last, that she would plead, "Nein, nein, bitte" ("No, no, please").

When Gretchen was naked, Schmidt ordered her to get on her knees. Before she could move, one of the guards forced her down. Schmidt told the other guard to throw some food on the floor in front of her. Then he ordered her to eat.

In spite of her fear and humiliation, Gretchen was grateful for the food. She scooped it up with both hands and shoved it into her mouth. Schmidt and the guards laughed.

Then Schmidt told Gretchen that she was a lucky Jew. Because she was so attractive, he had decided to give her preferential treatment. He would keep her healthy so she could maintain her looks. He would handle her like the prize animal that she was.

When Gretchen was finished with the food, Schmidt asked if she was still hungry. She was but didn't know what to say. Schmidt went to the table himself and threw more food in front of her. He said, "Here's a little more, but I want you to leave some room for dessert. Now, hurry up and eat." Gretchen did as she was told.

Schmidt then ordered the guards to wait outside. After they left, he started to unbutton his trousers. Gretchen was totally inexperienced in sex, but she sensed what was about to happen. She made her mind go blank. She felt Schmidt's hand forcing her head to and fro as he provided her with the dessert he had promised. He said, "Make sure to swallow it all. I don't want you to be hungry later."

That was the beginning of what would become Gretchen's regular routine. The tradeoff was that, unlike the rest of the camp's inmates, she remained strong and healthy. One other good thing was that, because of the Nazi law prohibiting sexual intercourse between Jews and so-called Aryans, Gretchen was never raped. Schmidt was a devout Nazi.

But Schmidt had other things planned for Gretchen. And they involved the rest of her family. One by one, he had her parents and brothers brought into his office to watch him and his guards move their hands all over Gretchen's naked body. He told her loves ones, "This is the last thing you will ever see." Then he shot each of them dead. Gretchen's agony was beyond comprehension.

Eventually, Schmidt tired of Gretchen. A new arrival had caught his fancy. Gretchen became part of the camp's general population. Now she had a different problem. The other inmates resented her for having been favored as the "commandant's little whore." A couple of other prisoners took pity on her and shared some food. But as their hunger increased, even they deprived her of her meager allotment.

By the time the camp was liberated, Gretchen was near death. It was then that she first saw the image of her guardian angel. When she gained enough strength, he taught her to call him Jack.

CHAPTER 7

After Tony composed himself, he went downstairs. His parents and brother were silent as their eyes were fixed on him.

Tony looked at Patrick and was about to speak. But before anything came out of his mouth, Patrick interrupted with a simple "I know." Nothing more had to be said.

Then, again showing concern for his baby sister, Tony asked, "Does Theresa know?" Angela answered, "Not yet." Tony became agitated, "Not yet?" He glared at his mother as he made his appeal, "There's no need for her to know about this. Why put her through it?" Angela came back at him, "For the same reason you went through it. It's what her grandmother wanted." Tony looked at his father and brother for support. Patrick said, "I agree with Tony." Pete added, "So do I."

Angela, visibly angry, raised her voice, "Theresa's stronger than you think. She's a grown woman, and she's having regular sex." She knew that would get to them. So what? It was about time they stopped regarding Theresa as their little puppy dog that needed protection. And Angela went on to tell them so.

Finally, they reached a compromise. They agreed to wait until after Theresa's upcoming marriage to tell her about Grandma's memoir. There was no reason to disrupt Theresa's enjoyment of preparing for her wedding.

Tony and Patrick stayed the night at their parents' house. It gave the four of them a feeling of comfort to be together. They all missed Theresa, but they would have to get used to that. She was now Billy's woman, and she would be spending her nights with *him*.

The next morning, after having breakfast with their parents, Tony and Patrick prepared to go home. Since Patrick lived nearby, he could stick around a while longer. But Tony had to get back to his condo in Virginia.

Patrick walked Tony to the car. After Tony got into the driver's seat, Patrick leaned over the open window and said, "We have some work to do." Tony responded, "That's for sure. I'll call you later today." Patrick stated, "I just hope the bastard's still alive." Tony replied, "So do I. Speak to you soon, bro."

When Patrick went back into the house, his father was alone in the living room. Angela was cleaning up in the kitchen. Pete said, "It was good to see Tony." Patrick responded, "Yeah, too bad it had to be under these circumstances." After a pause, Pete asked, "So what were you two talking about out there?" Patrick answered, "Nothing, just the usual bullshit." Pete looked into Patrick's face and repeated his son's words, "Just the usual bullshit." Patrick replied, "Yeah."

Both men became silent as Pete kept staring at Patrick. Finally, Patrick, getting uneasy, reacted, "What's with you, Dad? You're looking at me like I'm a perp." Pete asked, "Am I? Do you feel like a perp?" Patrick, increasingly uncomfortable, said, "Look, Dad, just tell me what's on your mind."

Pete diverted his gaze and sat down on the couch. He turned the TV on and raised the volume. He motioned with his head for Patrick to sit next to him. Speaking in a near whisper, Pete said, "That Schmidt guy is probably dead by now." Patrick agreed, "Yeah, probably." Pete went on, "But what if he's not?" Patrick just gave his father a blank look. Then Pete said, "I've been around, kid. I know why you asked Tony to get up here so fast. If that Nazi piece of shit is still alive, you want to get to him before he dies in his sleep." Patrick was about to talk, but Pete interrupted, "Don't try to snow me, Patrick. You may be a young hotshot at the department, but I've forgotten more than you'll ever know. You can take all those fancy books of yours and shove them up your ass."

In spite of the tense setting, Patrick couldn't help but get a kick out of his father's pique. Pete had long been frustrated by his lack of career advancement. He had to witness others, with more education and better test-taking ability, rise above him in spite of his innately superior skill at policing. Patrick knew his father was venting. But he also knew how proud Pete was of his two sons' success.

Patrick, realizing that his father was onto him and Tony, put forth, "He's probably dead. This whole conversation is much ado about nothing." Pete persisted, "But what if he's not?" Patrick gave his father another blank look. Pete touched Patrick's arm and told him, "Be careful, son. Don't do anything stupid."

Just then, Angela entered the room. She mentioned that the TV was so loud. Pete turned it off with the remote. Patrick stood up and announced that he was leaving. He said he had a hot date. He smiled at his mother and quipped, "Maybe this is the one. Then you can concentrate on Tony." Pete laughed at Patrick's good-natured mocking of Angela's concern over her sons' still being single. Angela reacted playfully, "You two, I don't know what I'll do with you."

After Patrick left, Angela and Pete stood facing each other in the living room. Pete knew her heart was still heavy with grief. He put his arms around her and kissed her on the lips. She looked at him and said, "You just might get lucky." Pete responded, "I wouldn't do that. What would Jack think if I took advantage of his little girl?" It was his way of telling Angela that he had finally allowed himself to let Theresa be an independent woman. Angela simply said, "I love you."

CHAPTER 8

Tony and Patrick didn't waste any time before starting on their quest. Initially, because Schmidt was such a common name, they went through loads of irrelevant information. However, with access to so many pertinent databases, they were able to narrow their search and pinpoint the individual they wanted.

After finding out that Schmidt had been declared a war criminal, the O'Brien twins were surprised to discover that his situation then changed. Inexplicably, he was admitted into the United States at just about the time his criminal status had been removed. Shortly after that, he seemed to have disappeared.

Tony, with his contacts in the federal government, was able to dig deeper. He learned that someone in the State Department, shortly after World War II, had intervened on Schmidt's behalf. Schmidt had been included in a group of Nazi war criminals whose past had been conveniently overlooked in return for their supposed help in combating Communism. Then they had been given identity changes after being allowed into the United States as legitimate immigrants. The reason for Schmidt's inclusion was actually his influential family ties in West Germany. He offered no value in fighting Communism. At any rate, he had entered the U.S. and taken on a new identity.

It was at this point that the twins hit a roadblock. Tony, who had been getting cooperation from his colleagues, suddenly was stonewalled. A sympathetic associate informed Tony that Schmidt (or whatever he was called now), if he was still alive, was being protected by elements within the federal government. It was too risky to acknowledge Schmidt's existence. Exposure of the program that had allowed him into the United States would be a major embarrassment and could cause a scandal.

Tony's buddy went on to say that there were powerful people who wouldn't be very happy to know that Tony had gotten as far as he had in his research. There was no way that Tony would be able to progress in his endeavor. His persistence could only hurt his career. There was absolutely nothing to gain and much to lose if he continued his efforts through governmental channels. But as a personal favor, Tony's pal agreed to try to at least determine if Schmidt was alive. In return, Tony swore to keep his friend anonymous in case the shit would ever hit the fan. To Tony's delight, it turned out that Schmidt was still among the living. Better yet, Tony's pal also provided Schmidt's current last name, Stone. But that was as far as things could go.

Now the O'Brien twins knew that Schmidt, using the last name Stone, was alive in the United States. But where in the United States? And Stone was such a common name. In effect, Tony and Patrick were back at square one. A database search revealed that there were hundreds of male Stones in their eighties in the U.S. Trying to find the right one would be like looking for a needle in a haystack.

Patrick and Tony were stymied. It would have been less frustrating to learn that Schmidt was dead. Knowing that he was still around but being unable to get to him was eating them up inside.

Patrick took a couple of vacation days to stay with Tony down in Virginia. They spent most of their time commiserating with each other at Tony's condo. While they were shooting the breeze and having a couple of beers, a light bulb went on in Tony's head. He looked at Patrick and said, "We may not be through yet." Patrick, who had been slouched on the living room couch, sat up and peered inquisitively at his brother. But Tony, obviously in deep thought, remained silent for a couple of seconds. Patrick, getting impatient, asked, "Would you like to share it with me, or is it a secret?" Tony was silent for another second. Then he let out, "Uncle Vic." Patrick reacted, "Wow, that *is* interesting."

CHAPTER 9

As had been his late father, Vic Tangredi was the black sheep of the family. Vic had followed in his dad's footsteps in organized crime. The Tangredi clan had long shunned both of them. The father/son combination represented a stain on the family name. To the rest of the proud, law-abiding Tangredis, the two of them were an embarrassment to the family and to all Italian-Americans, reinforcing a negative ethnic stereotype.

Vic had taken over his father's operation and expanded its influence. Whether one approved of him or not, Vic Tangredi was a successful, powerful man.

Virtually the only time the rest of the Tangredis mingled with Vic was at funerals. He was seldom invited to other family events. However, his late mother had been a close friend of Grandpa Jack's sister. And his wife was a pleasant, likable woman. In addition, Vic had two lovely daughters whose husbands were hard-working, respectable guys. So Vic's wife and daughters were well received and did stay in contact with the rest of the family. It was a somewhat strange situation. Oddly, Vic encouraged his spouse and children to "keep in touch with the uppity-ups." In spite of everything, Vic felt affection toward his relatives. He often told his wife, "Someday they'll need me. Then they won't be so uppity-up." Vic waited patiently for that day. In his mind, it would validate him to the rest of the family.

It only complicated matters that Vic's cousin Angela had married Pete O'Brien, part of a long line of law-enforcement members. The rare times the O'Brien twins and their sister had met Vic, he seemed like a great guy. He could be a real charmer. But the warmth he had shown toward them was genuine. Although he was their mother's cousin, not her brother, the kids had always referred to him as Uncle Vic.

Needless to say, the twins' type of work was not conducive to maintaining a relationship with Uncle Vic. And because of the indoctrination from their mother's side of the family, they had developed a psychological barrier toward him. Growing up, the mention of his name had been more or less taboo. That was why Tony and Patrick hadn't at first thought of enlisting Uncle Vic's help. Besides, they had believed that they could find Heinrich Schmidt through other sources.

Uncle Vic represented a possible new opportunity for the O'Brien boys. But they realized that seeking the services of organized crime would put them in bed with the enemy.

CHAPTER 10

Before Patrick had gone down to visit Tony, Pete told him, "If you two *are* going to do anything about Schmidt, I want to be in on it. Something like this has to be done right. It's one thing to get the guy. It's something else to get away with it. I don't want you making any mistakes."

Patrick responded, "I appreciate the offer, Dad, but in a way this doesn't concern you . . . at least not like it does Tony and me." Pete became incensed, "What the fuck are you talking about? Don't you think I know what would happen to you kids and your mother if crazy bastards like that ever took over? I thought about that just like you did when I read your grandmother's memoir. This is personal for me too."

Patrick apologized and promised to talk with Tony about it. Pete declared, "You're not just going to talk to him. You're going to tell him that this is the way it's going to be. Case closed."

When Patrick relayed Pete's message to Tony, the two brothers agreed that they didn't have much choice. And they had to admit that their father's assistance could be valuable. In fact, after deciding to request Uncle Vic's help, they realized that they would need a go-between to meet with the mobster. Given their law-enforcement positions, it wouldn't be prudent to be seen with their uncle. He was under constant surveillance.

Their father's status as a retired police officer could also be sticky. But since he was no longer on active duty, there would really be no repercussions. After all, Vic was his wife's cousin. It wouldn't be considered out of line for Pete, Vic, and their wives to socialize now that Pete's crime-fighting days were over.

Upon Patrick's return from Virginia, he briefed his father on the situation. Pete wasn't thrilled about associating with Vic Tangredi, but he had to agree that, under the circumstances, it made sense. Besides, it was at Pete's insistence that his sons were involving him.

When Pete suggested to Angela that they get together with Vic and his wife, she was surprised but receptive. Angela had never held hard feelings against Vic. She had just gone along with the rest of the family. She suspected that most of her generation of Tangredis had done the same. His exclusion had become a habit.

Angela called Vic's wife and arranged for the two couples to go out to dinner. They would then have dessert at Angela and Pete's house.

Vic Tangredi was a cynical man. He had to be in order to survive and prosper in his line of work. He readily agreed to get together socially with Angela and her "Irish cop," as Vic sometimes referred to Pete. But he thought to himself, "So I guess the uppity-ups need me for something."

CHAPTER 11

It was a little awkward when Pete and Angela met Vic and his wife Mary at the restaurant. Pete and Vic shook hands as the four of them waited for a table to become available.

Vic complained that the reservation should have been made in his name so they wouldn't have had to wait. Mary told him to calm down. But Vic remained annoyed. He was accustomed to being catered to.

When they were seated, the two couples engaged in small talk. Then Angela mentioned that she and Pete would like Mary and Vic to attend Theresa's wedding. Mary became visibly pleased. She knew that her husband was thrilled even if he was too proud to show it.

In order to hide his elation, Vic turned to sarcasm. Looking at Pete, he said, "Too bad I didn't make it to *your* wedding. I guess the invitation got lost in the mail." Pete fired back at him reflexively, "Fuck you, asshole, it wasn't me who didn't want you."

Vic Tangredi wasn't used to be spoken to like that. Ordinarily, he wouldn't have tolerated it. But under the circumstances, he swallowed his pride and responded, "Yeah, I guess I *am* acting like an asshole." Mary squeezed his hand under the table. She knew what an effort it was for him to restrain himself.

Angela interjected, "Come on, you two, behave yourselves." Pete, in an effort to be conciliatory, said, "I shouldn't have used that kind of language. I'm the asshole." Annoyed at Pete's continuing cursing, Angela snapped at him, "Will you stop!"

Before leaving the restaurant, the couples visited the restrooms. Pete and Vic used adjacent urinals. Looking straight ahead, Pete said, "You might be able to help me with something." Out of the corner of his eye,

Pete could see a smile come across Vic's face. In order to protect his dignity, Pete quickly added, "Actually, it's for my sons. We can talk later, away from the girls." Vic, knowing that Pete, like himself, was a proud man, ceased smiling and replied, "Sure, no problem. We'll pick our spot."

After eating dessert back at the house, Angela showed Mary around. The two women didn't push Vic to join them. They were relieved to see that he and Pete seemed to be bonding.

Pete took the opportunity to inform Vic about the Heinrich Schmidt matter and to ask if Vic could make any progress in locating the man. Vic responded that he might be able to and would certainly try. Pete asked what Vic would want in return. Vic, seeming genuinely hurt, told Pete, "Don't insult me. This is family. It'll be my pleasure to help nail that bastard."

When Pete asked how they would communicate, Vic told him, "Don't worry about that. I'll take care of it." Then Vic stated, "Maybe you should leave the whole thing to me. It's what I do. You guys are built to do just the opposite." Pete, looking dejected, replied, "Yeah, I know. I'm not happy about the boys' doing this, but they feel that they must. It's personal." Vic said, "I understand, but you guys are all about upholding the law. Justice and the law are two different things. When people can't get justice from the law, they rely on me to see to it that the score is settled."

Pete said that he would mention Vic's offer to Patrick and Tony. Then he added, "The boys and I appreciate your help. They feel kind of funny about not talking to you directly, but with their jobs and all that . . ." Vic responded, "It would be too risky for them. Tell them it's not a problem. Besides, it could also complicate things for me. It's best to handle it this way."

Before ending their talk, Pete said, "I won't even ask what kind of contacts you have." Vic replied, "Believe me, you don't want to know." Pete came back, "Oh, I believe you."

When Mary and Vic were about to leave, Vic said to Pete, "Now that you're retired from the cops, maybe you can work for me. I could use a guy with a pair of balls like yours." Pete smiled, "I don't think so, but thanks." It was the two men's way of expressing friendliness and respect for each other. They also knew that they would share the same fate later that night: a wifely reprimand for the behavior earlier at the restaurant.

CHAPTER 12

In a private moment during Theresa O'Brien's wedding, Vic Tangredi handed her father an envelope and said, "Here's the info you wanted." Then Vic asked, "Did you tell the boys about my offer?" Pete answered, "Yeah, they appreciate it, but they're a couple of stubborn bastards, just like their old man." Vic lowered his brow, "Okay, but tell them the offer still stands. Also, you and I can keep in touch in case they need any advice." Pete thanked Vic again for his help. Vic just grunted. Then he said, "At least they have you involved. That was a smart move."

Patrick and Tony each attended their sister's wedding without a date. Neither brother was serious about anyone, and they could sense that Uncle Vic might use the occasion to deliver the information for which they were waiting. Dates just would have been a distraction. They had arranged to stay at their folks' house after the wedding. That would give them time with their father to review things.

Tony and Patrick were standing together at the reception when Uncle Vic came over and shook their hands. They exchanged the usual polite greetings, and then Vic walked away. However, each twin had given him an extra-firm grip while peering into his eyes. And his return look had acknowledged their silent signal of thanks. Shortly after, their father joined them and gave a slight positive nod. They knew what that meant. The brothers waited impatiently for the festivities to end.

When they arrived home, Angela was tired and ready for bed. Pete and the boys decided to stay up and have a couple of beers. Angela mildly protested that they had already had enough to drink at the wedding. Pete joked that it was the Irish in them. The boys' enjoyment of beer was something they inherited from him. Angela retorted, "Yeah, all the bad stuff they got from *you*." Pete replied, "Of course."

Pete waited a few minutes after Angela went upstairs before checking on her. When he confirmed that she was asleep, he returned downstairs and announced, "Okay, let's take a look."

Upon glancing through the contents of the envelope, Pete and his sons all had the same reaction. Patrick spoke first, "It's scary." Tony stated, "We should put these guys in charge of national security." Pete joined in, "I can only imagine who's on their payroll. It *is* scary."

In Pete's hands was a list of names, addresses, phone numbers (listed, unlisted, unpublished), and birth dates of Harrison Stone (Heinrich Schmidt's current name) and some of his closest relatives. There were also several pages containing detailed biographical data and recent photos of each person on the list.

A feeling of guilt came over the three men. As much as they hated Heinrich Schmidt, they were invading the privacy of people who had nothing to do with his crimes.

But then Tony and Patrick reminded themselves of their grandmother's ordeal. They would make sure that no innocent person got hurt. However, Pete pointed out that losing a loved one certainly hurts. His sons would have to accept that killing Schmidt would cause pain to innocent people. There was no escaping that fact. Pete went on to say that Tony and Patrick were both decent men. If they were to go through with their act of revenge, would they be able to live with themselves?

Patrick complained to his father, "Don't try to talk us out of this. It has to be done." Referring to Schmidt's relatives, Patrick continued, "They'll get over it. Anyway, he's lived a long life."

Tony added, "What about our pain when we learned how Grandma suffered? If his family knew about this guy, they probably wouldn't blame us." Pete countered, "Maybe they do know." Tony came back at his father, "Then they deserve whatever they get if they still love the prick."

Moving on, Pete told his sons, "Vic asked me to repeat his offer to take care of this. It would make things so much easier and safer." Patrick responded, "But then we wouldn't be able to see the asshole suffer. It wouldn't be the same. I want the personal satisfaction."

Suddenly, the three of them were shocked to hear Angela's voice coming from the stairway, "Patrick's right; it wouldn't be the same." Before they could react, Angela told them that she hadn't really been asleep. She had suspected something fishy from the time Pete decided to socialize with Vic. And she had sensed that Pete and the twins would have something interesting to discuss when they wanted to stay up late.

To the O'Brien men's surprise, Angela was in complete accord with avenging her mother's agony. She shared Pete's concern about the risk involved, but she supported her sons' desire to handle things personally. Angela emphasized her feelings by saying, "Make sure he suffers. I want him to suffer."

At Angela's insistence, her husband and sons reluctantly shared with her the package Vic Tangredi had provided. But she agreed to be left unaware of the details involved with seeking retribution. Happily, she also concurred that Theresa should not know of Heinrich Schmidt's current existence.

Even Angela drew the line as to how much her daughter should be told. Pete and the boys were well-equipped professionals in dealing with this matter. Despite her previous rant against being overly protective of Theresa, Angela certainly didn't want her youngest child in any way involved.

At this point, it was still too early to think about logistics or specifics. It would take a while to get a lay of the land and devise an overall plan. And by now, everyone was tired. They all went upstairs to go to bed. However, each of them noted mentally that out of all the places in the United States, Harrison Stone and his immediate family lived in a town right near the O'Briens in Westchester County, just north of New York City.

CHAPTER 13

As expected, Theresa took it very hard when, after returning from her honeymoon, she read her grandmother's papers. Her family had decided to let her new husband see the memoir first. That turned out to be a wise move. Billy was able to empathize with Theresa, and he showed great tenderness and compassion when consoling her at her parents' home. Patrick and Tony also made sure to be there.

When they witnessed how Billy treated Theresa, the O'Brien twins gained a new perspective regarding their brother-in-law. He had come a long way from that punk kid who wanted to get into their sister's pants to her loving husband who provided the comfort she needed. Billy could sense the respect and affection from Theresa's brothers that he had always wanted. It felt good that he was no longer an outsider. He thought to himself, "I'm now one of them."

Before Billy took Theresa home, everybody agreed to get together again in about a month. It would be a good way to continue supporting each other. They set a date to have brunch at Angela and Pete's house on a Saturday. That way, Tony could drive up on Friday night, stay all day Saturday, and then rest part of Sunday before his return trip. The whole scenario was inconvenient for Tony, but it was worth it.

Time passed quickly, and the brunch weekend was upon them. It was late when Tony arrived at his folks' place. As he entered the house, he felt to confirm that he had his appointment book on him. He had all sorts of information in that little book, and he was almost paranoid about losing it. Although it didn't contain anything of earth-shattering importance, Tony had become dependent on it for quick reference.

His mother was already asleep, but his father had waited up. Both men were tired. After a quick fatherly greeting, they went upstairs. Tony started emptying his pockets before he even got to his bedroom. He fell asleep as soon as he hit the pillow.

The next morning, Tony took a quick shower before getting dressed. He had slept later than usual. He left his wallet and other personal items in his room and went downstairs.

Theresa and Billy were already at the house. Patrick was on his way. Angela and Pete were at the store buying eggs.

Billy and Theresa were in the living room. He was standing and looking out the window while she sat on the couch reading a magazine. When Theresa spotted her brother, she asked, "Tony, is this yours?" as she held up his appointment book. Before he could answer, she went on, "I found it in the hallway upstairs when I was going to Mom's room to get something. I figured it was probably yours. I was holding it for you." Tony was surprised as well as angry at himself for being so careless. He was glad that he hadn't been foolish enough to put anything about Heinrich Schmidt in there. He confirmed that the book was his and instinctively asked if Theresa had looked through it. She responded, "Of course I didn't look through it. What's in there anyway, some kind of nuclear secrets or just phone numbers of the hot chicks you're screwing?" Tony chided his sister, "Hey, what kind of talk is that?" Theresa shot back, "Loosen up, Tony. I'm a married woman who was living in sin." She put the appointment book on the coffee table and walked over to Billy. Feigning sexual arousal, she pressed against him and jested, "Let's do it right now, baby. I'm really in the mood." Billy, embarrassed, held Theresa by her shoulders. Tony conceded, "Okay, I get the message."

Theresa enjoyed giving her brother a hard time. Now that she was older and more mature, she liked to hold her own against him and his twin. She did her best to push their buttons.

Actually, Tony was pleased that Theresa was acting frisky. She appeared to be in good spirits, and evidently she was coping with the knowledge of Grandma Gretchen's ordeal. However, he still had his doubts over the decision to let Theresa know about it.

Tony took the appointment book from the coffee table and put it in his pocket. Then he picked up an attractive letter opener that was on the table. Theresa told him, "That was Grandma's. Mom said I could have it. That's what I was going to her room for when I found your little black book, the one with all the secrets." She kept up the sarcasm, "Billy, did you know that Tony is a big FBI man who carries around all the country's secrets?" Tony and Theresa smiled at each other. He jokingly said, "Have some respect for your elders, you little brat."

Billy casually added to the conversation. He mentioned to Theresa, "You sure took a long time up there." Theresa answered, "I didn't see the letter opener right away." He countered, "I thought your mother said it was on top of her desk. How long could it have taken you?" Theresa seemed a bit uncomfortable as she told her husband, "I also looked for my grandmother's memoir so I could read it again. But I couldn't find it." Theresa turned toward Tony, "Don't tell Mom I went through her drawers. I feel funny about that. It really wasn't right. Grandma's papers must be in Dad's dresser, but I certainly wasn't going to search *there*." Again, Theresa became playful, "Who knows what kind of masculine stuff I would have found? I might have been so shocked!"

To Theresa's surprise, Tony now reacted angrily, "That's enough. Knock off that kind of talk. Act like a lady." Theresa, noticeably hurt by Tony's tone, told him, "Gee, Tony, don't be so uptight. I was just kidding around." Tony, feeling guilty about upsetting Theresa, replied, "I know, but don't overdo it." He walked over and kissed her forehead.

Although he tended to worry more about Theresa than did Patrick, Tony wasn't ordinarily as demonstrative as his brother in showing affection toward her. That kiss had been unusual for Tony. But he felt compelled to relieve Theresa's pain, no matter how slight. He knew that regardless of how she acted, her brothers' approval was important to her.

Theresa's behavior didn't really bother Tony. His display of emotion was caused by consternation over how close she had come to discovering Heinrich Schmidt's dossier. Tony knew that it was lying, together with Grandma Gretchen's memoir, under some shirts in his father's dresser. He shuddered to think what would have happened had Theresa found it?

Tony also wasn't happy that Theresa had wished to re-read Grandma Gretchen's papers. He didn't want his sister dwelling on them. Although there was nothing he could do about it at this point, he now totally regretted having acquiesced on letting Theresa see them. Tony had been surprised at how strong and vindictive his mother turned out to be. But he remembered how sensitive Theresa had been as a child. In spite of the wise-guy persona she liked to portray, he knew that her psyche was still fragile. He could perceive how even now she was sulking after his scolding of her.

This little unpleasant encounter was forgotten as the weekend progressed. Overall, the family get-together was enjoyable and proved to be a healing experience. Everyone agreed to make it a regular occurrence. However, the O'Brien twins' desire for retribution remained intact.

CHAPTER 14

After studying the data on Harrison Stone and his relatives, Patrick came up with a way to indirectly get close to Grandma Gretchen's tormentor. It revolved around Stone's 25-year-old granddaughter.

Things seemed to be falling into place perfectly. First, Stone and his kin resided nearby. In addition, Stone's granddaughter Debbie had an interest in antiques. Coincidentally, so did Patrick's sister, Theresa. Coming up soon was a local outdoor antiques fair. There was a good chance Debbie Stone would attend. Patrick knew that Theresa intended to be there. He would go along and if need be, use her help in meeting Debbie Stone.

Patrick shared his plan with his father and brother. The only reservation was expressed by Tony. He cautioned Patrick about being attracted to Debbie Stone. Tony pointed out that she resembled Susan, Patrick's ex-fiancee. Patrick scoffed at Tony's concern. But then Pete noted that merely getting friendly with one or more of Stone's relatives could complicate things. However, the three of them eventually agreed on using Patrick's idea. Thus far, they had no other course of action. If Debbie Stone failed to visit the antiques fair, they would go back to the drawing board.

Sure enough, Patrick spotted Debbie at the fair. He asked Theresa to strike up a conversation with her. It was easy to do since people were casually moving about as they viewed the display tables. It was a very relaxed, informal setting.

Theresa jokingly told Patrick to get his own girls. She continued jocularly, "So this is why you came with me: to pick up girls. How crass! And I thought you wanted to expand your horizons and get a little culture. Okay, I'll do it, but you owe me, especially if you get laid." Patrick gave his sister a look of exasperation. She returned a mischievous smile before strolling to where Debbie was looking at a piece of pottery. Before long, the two women were talking, and Patrick nonchalantly walked over. Theresa introduced him and Debbie. When Theresa saw that they took to each other, she gradually backed away to another table.

Patrick realized that Tony had been right about being attracted to Debbie. Patrick thought to himself, "Under different circumstances, I could really go for her." He could also easily sense that the attraction was mutual. Debbie was the one who hinted that they could get together later if Patrick was free. Everything seemed to be moving at lightning speed. Before either of them knew it, they were planning to go to a movie that evening and have dinner the following weekend.

CHAPTER 15

As Patrick drove to Debbie's place, he wondered how such a sweet thing could be descended from a monster like Harrison Stone. He was careful to now think of and talk about the man by his current name. It had been Patrick's father who suggested that they do so. It was important from here on not to mention the name Heinrich Schmidt. That could really screw things up.

Patrick didn't know what to do about his feelings toward Debbie. He had already started down the slippery slope. He decided just to allow things to happen. He also had to be careful not to let on that he already knew facts about her and her family.

Debbie had a nice little apartment not far from her parents' expensive house. When Patrick brought her back to her place after the movie, there was an awkward pause at the front door. They both wanted to end the night with a sensual kiss, but Patrick was torn over the whole situation. Finally, he rationalized that he should go for it. Otherwise, Debbie might get suspicious. It was the perfect excuse to give in to his desires.

Debbie and Patrick looked longingly at each other before briefly locking lips and making contact with their tongues. As he was about to leave, Debbie said, "Oh, I almost forgot. I mentioned you to my mother, and she suggested that we could join my family for dinner next weekend at my parents' house. My cousins will be in from out of town." Patrick was silent and obviously taken aback. Upon seeing his reaction, Debbie became disconcerted and started to jabber, "I told her it was a bad idea. You would feel pressured. It's too soon for something like that. We're just getting acquainted. I'm sorry. I'm so embarrassed."

Patrick attempted to calm her down, "No, don't be embarrassed. I'm flattered. It sounds great." He silently told himself that this would facilitate getting to Debbie's grandfather. But although he refused to think about it, his deeper concern right then was Debbie's despair. He wanted to comfort her. He compulsively took her in his arms and plunged his tongue into her mouth. At first, she reciprocated with equal vigor. Then, having just met earlier that day, she gently freed herself from Patrick's grasp. He understood totally.

Patrick told Debbie he would call her during the week to confirm directions and the time of the dinner. Before entering the elevator, he glanced back at Debbie's door. It was still open with her standing there. They exchanged departing smiles.

When Patrick briefed his brother and father on his progress with Debbie, he left out the more intimate details and his feelings toward her. But Patrick and Tony could always read each other perfectly. When the two of them were alone together, Tony gave Patrick an I-told-you-so admonishment.

Patrick didn't try to deny his feelings toward Debbie. With Tony, it would have been useless. But Patrick asserted that his hatred for Harrison Stone was undiminished. He assured his brother that he could compartmentalize his emotions. Patrick insisted that he could have it both ways. He could date this great girl while simultaneously advancing toward avenging Grandma Gretchen's suffering. He would enjoy Debbie for as long as things lasted. They would then go their separate ways.

Tony reluctantly accepted his sibling's argument, but he didn't really buy it. Romance was one area where the O'Brien twins differed. Tony was pretty much the love-'em-and-leave-'em type while his brother tended to be sentimental and prone to commitment. Tony hoped for the best, but he knew in his gut that Patrick was deluding himself.

There was now a major complication. Besides fretting over how it would affect their mission, Tony feared for his brother's psychological well-being. Patrick would be burdened with guilt no matter how things turned out. He would be torn between finding justice for his grandmother and causing pain to Debbie.

Although Tony didn't allow it to come to the surface, he also worried, deep down, how Patrick's involvement with Debbie would affect his own emotions and the O'Brien brotherly bond. Tony realized that, at a certain point, he might have to go it alone in seeking retribution. If so, at best, it would put a strain on his relationship with Patrick.

CHAPTER 16

Debbie sensed that Patrick was uneasy when he came to pick her up. She hoped it was because he was worried about making a favorable impression on her family. She was still concerned about perhaps pushing things too fast. They were going to have dinner at her parents' home, on their second date, after only knowing each other for a week. Even if he wouldn't say it, maybe Patrick had a problem with that. It was inevitable that her relatives would assume something serious between them, and he might become the center of attention.

Debbie told Patrick that, if he wanted to, they could leave her parents' house early. She would say that she didn't feel well. Patrick asked, "Why would I want to leave early?" Debbie answered, "I don't know. But just in case you do, it's okay. I don't want you to be uncomfortable." Patrick smiled and touched her face. He said, "I won't be uncomfortable as long as I'm with *you*." Debbie returned his smile and impulsively gave him a quick, soft kiss on the lips. She was embarrassed as they awkwardly looked at each other for a second or two. Then she said, "We better get going."

When Patrick entered the home of Debbie's parents, her mother greeted him warmly and introduced him to everybody as Debbie's friend. The situation was surreal for Patrick as, preceding the introductions, he already recognized some of the people.

As if part of a dramatic script, the last person to meet Patrick was Debbie's grandfather. Patrick felt his heart thumping and experienced a pounding in his head as he watched the right hand of Harrison Stone extend toward him from the wheelchair in which Stone was sitting. Stone also had an oxygen tube inserted in his nostrils. His dossier had revealed that he suffered from arthritis and emphysema, but apparently both ailments were more severe than had been indicated.

As he grasped Stone's hand, Patrick thought how that same hand had years ago held Grandma Gretchen's head. A feeling of revulsion came over the O'Brien twin. He felt almost faint. Noticing his look of distress, Debbie asked if he was all right. Recovering quickly, Patrick answered that he had felt a sneeze coming on, but it had passed.

During a moment alone together, Debbie mentioned to Patrick that both of her grandfather's afflictions were worsening. It had only been recently that he periodically started using a wheelchair and oxygen tube. Some days were better than others, but it was obvious that he was gradually getting weaker. Watching him deteriorate broke her heart. He was such a loving and kind person.

Patrick, resisting the urge to expose the "real" Harrison Stone, changed the subject. He realized that he would have to condition himself to see and discuss the hated figure without displaying anger.

Ironically and paradoxically, after observing Stone in this state and knowing Debbie's feelings, Patrick would also have to guard against being lulled into sympathy toward the old man. Patrick decided to remind himself of Grandma Gretchen whenever he might be tempted to relent in his resolve for justice.

Somehow, Patrick managed to act natural as he spent a "pleasant" evening with Debbie's relatives. They all seemed like lovely people, including the individual Patrick loathed. If he didn't know better, Patrick would have thought that Harrison Stone was a really nice guy.

Patrick also noted that Stone didn't have a trace of a foreign accent. However, that didn't surprise Patrick. He had assumed that Stone had taken an English-immersion course as part of the assimilation process. From all appearances, Harrison Stone was a typical American.

When Debbie and Patrick got back to her place, they gave each other a passionate kiss at her front door. Their tongues swirled around each other as their bodies pressed together.

Strangely, Patrick was thinking about Tony. Patrick envied his brother for being able to remain emotionally aloof from his dates regardless of how attracted he was to them.

In spite of how horny Patrick was getting, he was actually relieved when Debbie backed away from him. She said, "I hope you don't mind, but it's still too soon." Patrick responded, "No problem, I understand." Then Debbie asked, "Will you call me?" Patrick answered, "Of course. I'll call you in a couple of days, and we'll set something up for next weekend. That is, if you're free." Her immediate response was "Absolutely."

On the drive home, Patrick made his mind go blank. There was too much for him to absorb. He couldn't wait to get to sleep and become unconscious.

CHAPTER 17

Aware that Patrick was dating Debbie, Theresa was naturally curious about how serious things were getting. But when Theresa questioned Patrick, he was reticent. Besides all the other intrigue, he was reluctant to allow himself to become hooked on someone. He hated the thought of going through another broken relationship.

Although, there was a definite difference between Susan, his ex-fiancee, and Debbie. With Susan, Patrick had always seemed to be in pursuit of her affection. She had been a bit of a prima donna. Debbie, on the other hand, openly showed her desire to be with Patrick.

Theresa, mindful of Patrick's disappointing experience with Susan, didn't push the issue. She had the good sense not to risk hitting a nerve. But Theresa's questioning prompted Patrick to realistically consider the consequences of his involvement with Debbie. The more he did, the guiltier he felt. He was obviously using Debbie as they continued to see each other. Eventually, she would suffer the pain for which he was setting her up. But that wasn't all that was bothering Patrick. He had to admit to himself that he was falling in love with her. He was also setting *himself* up for a fall.

Ever since meeting Debbie, Patrick had assumed that a certain revelation would abruptly terminate their relationship. Once he would make known his Jewish roots, her family, if not she herself, would put an end to things. Attitudes and beliefs get passed down from generation to generation. So it would be with the Stones, whose patriarch had a history of very strong beliefs and attitudes indeed.

However, during a conversation about her grandfather, Debbie said something very surprising and confusing to Patrick. She was mentioning how the old man, a devout Catholic, went to church practically every day to make confession. He had long ago divulged to his family that he had deep feelings of guilt regarding his past. In fact, he attributed his increasingly severe emphysema and arthritis to being punished by God for previous misdeeds. Harrison Stone almost welcomed the diseases as a form of penance. As a dying old man, he worried more and more about his soul's salvation. He also told his family that he hoped he would get a chance in heaven to ask for forgiveness from people he had hurt. But he steadfastly refused to go into further detail.

Debbie went on to say that her grandfather often read the Bible and frequently called his close friend, a rabbi now living in Chicago, to discuss certain passages. Patrick could hardly believe his ears. But it was obvious that Harrison Stone, somewhere along the line, had undergone a spiritual transformation. Perhaps it had something to do with the rabbi.

Out of curiosity, if nothing else, Patrick couldn't hold out. He mentioned to Debbie that his grandmother, a Jew, had converted to Catholicism after marrying his grandfather. Debbie's only reaction was to say that her mother, a former Protestant, had become a Catholic upon her engagement to Debbie's father.

The next time Patrick was at Debbie's parents' home, her mother noted that it was a coincidence that both his family and theirs had Catholic converts. Harrison Stone, who was also present, joked that his rabbi friend would be happy to hear that Debbie was going out with someone who was part Jewish. Patrick was staggered.

Still brimming with curiosity, on the drive back to Debbie's place, Patrick asked her how her grandfather and the rabbi had become so friendly. She told him that when her grandfather was thirty years old, he was in a car accident. Rabbi Joe, as Debbie's family referred to him, pulled her grandfather from the car just before it exploded. Then Rabbi Joe, a total stranger at the time, covered her grandfather with his own body as burning debris came flying at them. They wound up in the hospital together and formed a strong attachment.

Debbie also disclosed her grandfather's expressed hope that Rabbi Joe perhaps had saved his soul as well as his life. But that would be decided by God. At any rate, Rabbi Joe's act of courage had profoundly affected her grandfather. The two men became even closer after their wives died. They provided solace to each other. When Rabbi Joe moved to take over a congregation in Chicago, he and Harrison Stone remained dear friends. After retirement, Rabbi Joe stayed in Chicago in order to be near his children. But he and Debbie's grandfather spoke regularly with each other over the phone.

When Patrick left Debbie off at her apartment, his head was spinning. He kept reminding himself of what Harrison Stone had done to Grandma Gretchen and her previous family. Patrick was forcing himself to continue to hate the old man. But he realized how ironic it was that Stone's death would cause great sorrow to a rabbi.

Tony's concern for Patrick's psyche had been well-founded. Now there was an additional twist. Harrison Stone was filled with remorse over his past. In addition to his physical suffering, the man was enduring great psychological pain. Killing him would relieve him of both.

Patrick wasn't sure what to say at his upcoming meeting with Tony and their father. All he knew was that Tony was becoming impatient.

CHAPTER 18

Tony wasn't the only one who was losing patience. Angela, despite having agreed to stay out of the details, started bugging Pete about the mission's progress. She could sense that Patrick might be lost to the cause.

Patrick had reluctantly informed his mother about his relationship with Debbie. Although not thrilled, Angela was taking it surprisingly well. She understood that the family of her mother's tormentor couldn't be held responsible for his actions. And Angela didn't want to interfere with her son's love life. After all, she was always urging her boys to find the right girl. If Debbie turned out to be the one for Patrick, so be it. Angela was willing to bite the bullet and embrace her.

But Angela's hatred for Debbie's grandfather remained as strong as ever. Angela was still counting on Tony to carry out the retribution.

However, Tony was wrestling with his own problems. As much as he tried to suppress it, the mental image of the sickly old man in Harrison Stone's recent photo remained. It was hard to feel the same intensity that had enveloped Tony toward the swaggering Nazi scum described in Grandma Gretchen's memoir. Tony kept reminding himself that Harrison Stone and Grandma's torturer were the same person.

Needless to say, when Patrick apprised his brother and father of Harrison Stone's troubled conscience and friendship with Rabbi Joe, it exacerbated Tony's ambivalence. The two brothers now shared a sense of guilt for wavering on seeking justice for their grandmother.

During the latest meeting with his sons, Pete O'Brien, for the most part, remained silent. He let the boys express themselves. Then he suggested that they end the session so each of them could spend some time alone to think things over. They could talk again at the next family get-together in a couple of weeks. With still no concrete plan, another two weeks wouldn't make much difference. But Pete urged Tony and Patrick to be ready next time to either have firmer ideas for moving forward or to let the situation rest. Pete ended the meeting by telling his sons to contemplate how Harrison Stone, both physically and mentally, was suffering. Would killing him be punishment *or* relief from his ordeal?

CHAPTER 19

Instead of the usual family brunch, the O'Briens decided to have dinner together for this particular bonding session. It was the middle of the summer, and they would be eating when it was still light out. They might even sit on the deck. The weather was beautiful.

Angela and Theresa spent most of the afternoon with each other shopping. Billy was playing softball with his buddies. It gave Pete, Patrick, and Tony the perfect opportunity to share their thoughts and emotions in private.

The three men placed themselves in a small room off the corner of the finished basement. That room had always been the favorite spot for the O'Brien children to discuss important matters with their parents. It was only natural that they would gravitate toward it for this monumental occasion.

Pete let his sons do most of the talking. In his role as facilitator, he encouraged them to be completely open. But he also expressed his own feelings. The hours passed by quickly as they bared their souls. The experience was draining for all of them. When they were finally spent emotionally, mentally, and physically, they fell silent for several minutes until they regained their strength and were ready to resume.

Pete and the boys knew that now was decision time. It was also clear that either choice would be flawed. It would be difficult for Tony and Patrick to cope no matter which way they would go. The situation was especially complicated for Patrick. He had just confirmed what had already become apparent: his love for Debbie. Despite Patrick's objection, Tony insisted on being the sole executioner if that was the direction they would choose. Pete agreed with Tony. It would be untenable for Patrick to be in love with the granddaughter of someone he had murdered.

Then Pete warned that it would also be hard for Tony to deal with committing the act. Tony was a decent person who wasn't wired to be a killer. Regardless of the motive, it just wasn't in him. Uncle Vic had been correct about that.

Tony argued that he would feel guilty for the rest of his life if he failed to avenge Grandma Gretchen's suffering. Pete came back at him, "You know what the old bastard's going through. Besides the physical pain, he's consumed by guilt. He's a pathetic tortured soul. That's his punishment. To kill him would just put him out of his misery."

At that moment, Angela and Theresa, having returned from shopping, came into the room. Angela said, "So there you are. We were wondering where you all were hiding." Then she asked, "Who's the pathetic tortured soul who would be put out of his misery?" Pete, thinking fast, replied, "We were having a discussion on capital punishment." Angela retorted, "You've always been in favor of capital punishment. It sure didn't sound that way just now." Pete, again thinking fast, "I'm having second thoughts."

Theresa chimed in, "Daddy's getting soft in his old age." She told her mother, "Come on, Mom, let's leave the male chauvinist pigs alone. They may say something too delicate for us womenfolk to hear." Pete addressed his sons, "You know, boys, that baby sister of yours is becoming more and more of a wise-ass." Theresa stuck out her tongue at her father. Then, just before leaving with her mother, she gave him that smile that always made his heart melt.

Angela, once upstairs, realized that she had forgotten to get something at one of the stores. She drove back there and left her daughter at the house to watch a television show. Theresa turned on the small TV in the kitchen.

Meanwhile, the O'Brien men remained silent for several minutes. They wanted to be sure Angela and Theresa were out of earshot. Finally, Patrick said to Tony, "You know, bro, Dad's right. We would be cutting off our nose to spite our face. We're not murderers. Hell, we protect people from murderers."

Tony looked at his father and said, "You knew all along that this was how it would wind up. You never intended to let us go through with it. You old fox." Pete responded, "It would have been terrible. But I had to let you kids see for yourselves. You can have the satisfaction of knowing that he suffers every day."

Pete told his sons that he wanted to leave them alone with each other for a while. When he got upstairs, Theresa informed him that Angela had gone back to the store and would return soon. She added that Billy should also be arriving shortly. Pete told Theresa that she would be more comfortable watching the large-screen television. He turned off the small TV in the kitchen, and they both went into the living room.

Theresa said to her father, "Daddy, I hope you don't think I was acting fresh a little while ago. I was just kidding around." Pete kissed her forehead and said, "Of course not. I guess you inherited your mother's sense of humor, just like your brothers."

Then Pete walked out to the hallway between the living room and kitchen. He kneeled down and lifted a little lid at the foot of the wall. He told his sons, through a narrow chute that extended down to that small room in the basement, to come upstairs soon for dinner.

The meal and chatting that followed were very pleasant. But the O'Brien men waited impatiently for Theresa and Billy to leave. The difficult task of informing Angela about the decision to let Harrison Stone live would take place that night.

As her sons and husband had feared, Angela, although not really surprised, did not take the news well. She told them she had suspected "the worst" after overhearing part of the supposed "capital punishment" discussion earlier in the basement. Then she warned, "If you don't take care of it, maybe someone else will." Pete became alarmed, "Don't do anything crazy, Angie."

After Tony and Patrick left, Pete held Angela in his arms before leading her to the living room couch. Holding her hand, he went through the entire scenario he had reviewed with their sons. Reluctantly, Angela acquiesced. She would console herself with the knowledge of how Harrison Stone was suffering.

The next day, Pete relayed Angela's professed concession to Patrick and Tony. All three of them were relieved. However, Angela's obvious threat from the previous night lingered in their minds. Was her compliance sincere?

CHAPTER 20

Patrick and Debbie continued to date until the inevitable happened: they became engaged. Angela seemed to be handling the situation. Debbie and her parents were lovely people. Miraculously, Angela even managed to act friendly toward Harrison Stone when circumstances called for her to do so. She did it for Patrick's sake. Her sons and husband realized how difficult that was for her. It was hard enough for *them*. They knew she didn't buy into the concept that Stone's tortured existence was adequate punishment for his past. Pete was still uneasy about what she might do.

But Angela wasn't the only one Pete should have been worried about. Tony was finding it hard to live with himself. Besides the guilt he felt toward Grandma, he was ashamed every time his mother looked at him. She had been staring straight at him that night when she had blurted, "If you don't take care of it, maybe someone else will." He knew she had expected him to carry things out alone after Patrick's involvement with Debbie.

Tony realized how easy it would be to get away with killing Harrison Stone. All someone would have to do was catch the old man in a secluded setting, pull out the oxygen tube, and threaten him. The guy would probably drop dead from fright before the emphysema finished him off.

It was at Debbie and Patrick's engagement party that Tony decided, "It's time to shit or get off the pot." The event was being held at Debbie's parents' big house with a large crowd. Everyone knew that Harrison Stone often stayed by himself in a small room in the basement. He liked to be there with his thoughts. It also allowed him, without disturbing others, to deal with the pain when the arthritis would act up. To get to and from the basement, Stone utilized the elevator his son and daughter-in-law had installed for him after he had moved in with them a few years ago.

The room also was where Harrison Stone used to spend hours sitting and talking with Rabbi Joe. Stone was particularly depressed this day. He had hoped his old friend could attend Debbie's engagement party. But the rabbi was too ill to travel. Stone knew that Rabbi Joe's days, like his own, were numbered.

After not finding Harrison Stone upstairs, Tony nonchalantly made his way toward the door leading to the basement. As he descended the steps, he was still torn. He would say that he had gone down to check on the old man and found him dead. No one would suspect foul play. But could Tony go through with it?

Surprisingly, Tony heard voices coming from Harrison Stone's special room. Suddenly, there was a loud groan. That was followed by "Nein, nein, bitte." Then there was another loud groan.

Tony rushed toward the commotion. When he opened the door, he saw the lifeless Harrison Stone lying in a pool of blood. The killer, standing over the body and holding the murder weapon, calmly turned toward Tony and declared, "*Somebody* had to do it."

Besides being shocked, Tony was baffled. He started to silently ask himself, "How . . . ?" But at this point, what did it matter? All he knew was that his mother's warning had come true.

Eventually, Tony would be made aware of the two key factors that hadn't been considered. The first was the *unacknowledged* discovery of Heinrich Schmidt's dossier in Pete O'Brien's dresser. The second was the chute between the hallway and basement at Tony's parents' house. When Tony and his siblings were growing up, the chute had provided a convenient way for them to communicate. Years later, it would serve as the perfect vehicle for eavesdropping.

As Tony stared at the murder weapon, he understood its symbolism. Firmly gripping her grandmother's bloody letter opener, Theresa looked deeply into her brother's eyes and said, "Now Grandma can rest in peace."